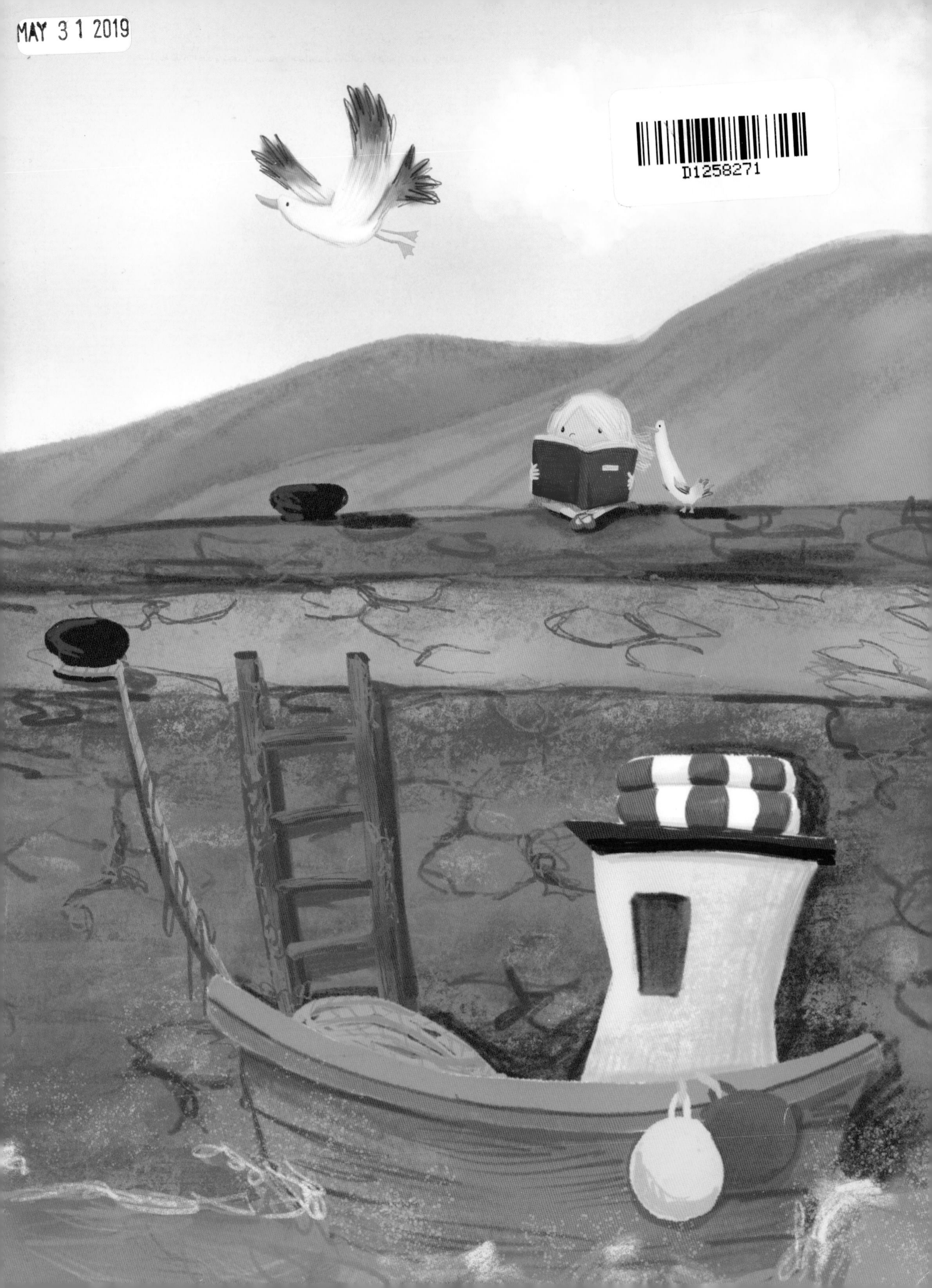

The
Sketchbook

JULIA SEAL

PETER PAUPER PRESS, INC.
White Plains, New York

Designed by Heather Zschock

Published by Peter Pauper Press, Inc.
202 Mamaroneck Avenue
White Plains, New York 10601 USA

Published in the United Kingdom and Europe by Peter Pauper Press, Inc.
c/o White Pebble International
Unit 2, Plot 11 Terminus Rd.
Chichester, West Sussex PO19 8TX, UK

Library of Congress Cataloging-in-Publication Data

Names: Seal, Julia, author, illustrator.
Title: The sketchbook / by Julia Seal.
Description: First edition. | White Plains, New York : Peter Pauper Press,
Inc., 2019. | Summary: Lily's love of drawing is muted by her shyness and
fear of what others might think, but when a gust of wind whips up the
pages in her sketchbook suddenly everything changes.
Identifiers: LCCN 2018046364 | ISBN 9781441329370 (hardcover)
Subjects: | CYAC: Drawing--Fiction. | Bashfulness--Fiction.
Classification: LCC PZ7.1.S336885 Sk 2019 | DDC [E]--dc23 LC record available at https://lccn.loc.gov/2018046364

ISBN 978-1-4413-2937-0
Manufactured for Peter Pauper Press, Inc.
Printed in Hong Kong

7 6 5 4 3 2 1

Visit us at www.peterpauper.com

For Joseph and Amalie

Lily loved to draw.

She began drawing as soon
as she woke up...

...and continued drawing late into the night.

She drew at the kitchen table,

and on the train.

in the park,

Where others saw the ordinary,
Lily had a special way of
seeing the *extraordinary*.

But Lily was shy and afraid of what
others might think of her drawings,
so she kept her pictures hidden
in her sketchbook.

As the seagulls circled above,
Lily wondered what it would be like
to see the world so differently—
the way only birds can.

Lily especially liked to draw other children.

Sometimes she'd even draw herself
joining in with them.

Today the children were searching
for crabs in the
harbor's rock pools.

"What do crabs actually do when they are hidden under the sea?" wondered Lily.

She drew a crab. Then she added a top hat and tap-dancing shoes.

"I will call you Bob," she decided.

Just then, the wind began to pick up.
The boats clinked and clanked as they moved
up and down with the splashing waves.

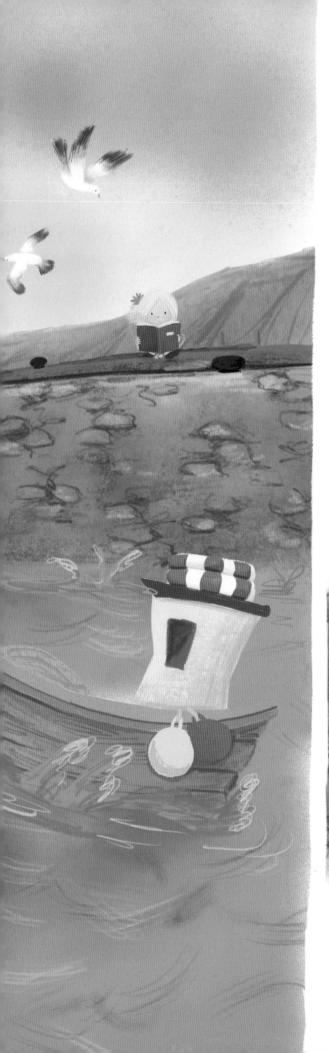

"I'd better go!" said Lily.

She gazed at Bob the crab.
"I will draw a friend for you
tomorrow," she promised.

But, as Lily hopped off the dock,
her feet slipped on the damp stones.
Her sketchbook flew out of her hands
and tumbled to the ground!

A gust of wind whipped up the pages, twirling them into the air . . .

...swirling,

curling,

flying away,

just out of reach!

"My pictures!" gasped Lily.

People stared. Children pointed. Tears rolled down Lily's face. She grabbed what was left of her sketchbook and turned to run away.

But then Lily noticed something. People were smiling!

"Is this my boat?
I never noticed
how grand she looks!"
the fisherman
exclaimed.

"This looks like my Charlie.
I do miss him,"
sighed a village lady.
"May I keep this?"

"Is that a tap-dancing crab?"
asked the children. They giggled.

Everyone crowded
around Lily.

"Did you draw all these?"

"They are wonderful!"

"You are quite an artist!"

And—for the first time in Lily's life,
words came spilling out of her!

Twirling,

swirling,

flying,

free!

The children came closer to listen.

"That's Bob," Lily explained to them.
"He's a crab that has taken up tap-dancing because
he has a lot of legs and he's really rather good."

The children laughed.

"Can we see your other pictures?" they asked.

"Yes!" she exclaimed.

Each one of her drawings had a story—
told in a special way that only Lily could tell it.

And now she'd found a voice,
and friends to share them with.